High Mountains
Starlight Caves
Rainbow Pools
Huts
Ice Owls
Burning Bushes
Lake
Sledging Slopes
Gardens
School
Kennels
Ridge
Husky Training Ground
Fields
LAND OF ICE AND WINTER

Linda Chapman lives in Leicestershire with her family and two dogs. When she is not writing, she spends her time looking after her three children, reading, talking to people about writing, and horse riding whenever she can.

You can find out more about Linda on her websites at *lindachapman.co.uk* and *lindachapmanauthor.co.uk*

Books by Linda Chapman

BRIGHT LIGHTS
CENTRE STAGE
MY SECRET UNICORN series
NOT QUITE A MERMAID series
SKATING SCHOOL series
SKY HORSES series
STARDUST series
UNICORN SCHOOL series

Linda Chapman

Illustrated by Nellie Ryan

PUFFIN

Madam Letsworth's Magic Ice-Skating Academy

ICE OWLS
AMANDA
ZOE
HEATHER
TASHA
OLIVIA
SNOW FOXES
CAMILLA
TESS
CLARE
HELENA
EMILY

To Lindsey Heaven, who first had the brilliant idea of a skating school in a magic land, and because she loves the characters as much as I do!

PUFFIN BOOKS

Published by the Penguin Group
Penguin Books Ltd, 80 Strand, London WC2R ORL, England
Penguin Group (USA) Inc., 375 Hudson Street, New York, New York 10014, USA
Penguin Group (Canada), 90 Eglinton Avenue East, Suite 700, Toronto, Ontario, Canada M4P 2Y3
(a division of Pearson Penguin Canada Inc.)
Penguin Ireland, 25 St Stephen's Green, Dublin 2, Ireland (a division of Penguin Books Ltd)
Penguin Group (Australia), 250 Camberwell Road, Camberwell, Victoria 3124, Australia
(a division of Pearson Australia Group Pty Ltd)
Penguin Books India Pvt Ltd, 11 Community Centre, Panchsheel Park, New Delhi – 110 017, India
Penguin Group (NZ), 67 Apollo Drive, Rosedale, North Shore 0632, New Zealand
(a division of Pearson New Zealand Ltd)
Penguin Books (South Africa) (Pty) Ltd, 24 Sturdee Avenue, Rosebank, Johannesburg 2196, South Africa

Penguin Books Ltd, Registered Offices: 80 Strand, London WC2R ORL, England

puffinbooks.com

First published 2010

A ...

ISBN: 978-0-141-32633-7

www.greenpenguin.co.uk

Penguin Books is committed to a sustainable future for our business, our readers and our planet. The book in your hands is made from paper certified by the Forest Stewardship Council.

Contents

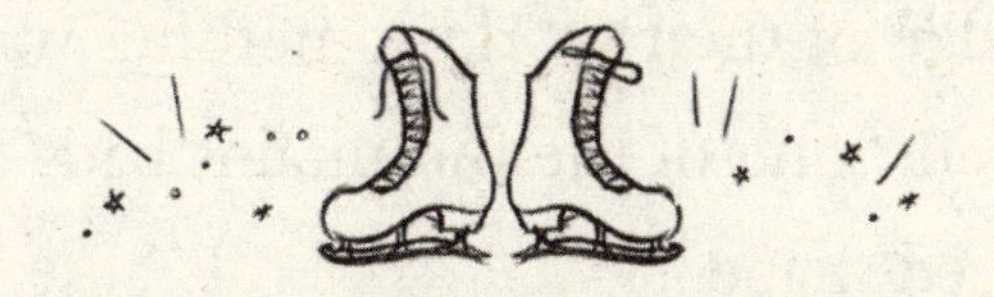

In the Magic Land of Ice and Winter . . .

Everything looked just as it always did. A blanket of crisp snow covered the fields and meadows, towns and villages. Frozen lakes glittered in the rays of the pale sun and a mist hung over the tops of the jagged mountains. Silvery robins darted from tree to tree while white fluffy fox cubs tumbled after each other. The ice sylphs who lived in the land went about their business as usual. But at the edge of their world something was different: one of the mountains had changed shape.

Something lay curled around it, great wings folded flat. Dark-red scaly sides moved in and out and the steam from its breath formed thick clouds in the icy air . . .

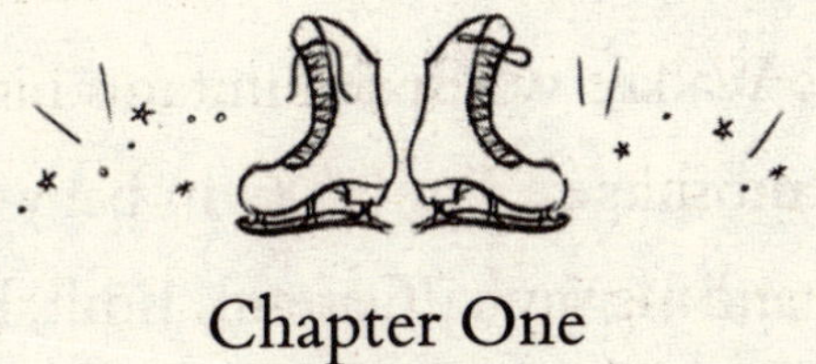

Chapter One
Emily

Ten-year-old Emily Walker spun round in her socks on the kitchen floor, one arm above her head, her shoulder-length chestnut-brown hair swinging round her face. She wished she was ice-skating, then she would have been able to twirl without stopping. If she could have anything in the whole world, it would be to have proper skating lessons and to have her own ice-skating dress and boots.

Mrs Walker was spooning food into the open mouths of Emily's twin baby sisters, Rose and Jasmine. 'Careful, Em!' she said, grabbing the dish as Emily's outstretched hand knocked against it and jolted a dollop of green mush across the table.

'Sorry, Mum,' Emily said. Jasmine smiled at her, and Rose pointed and said, 'A-ga.'

Mrs Walker sighed and rubbed her hand across her forehead, leaving a smudge of baby food. Emily noticed how tired her mum looked. 'Do you want me to help?' she offered.

'Thanks, love,' her mum said gratefully. 'If you finish feeding them, I can get the washing on.'

Emily sat down and started to feed the twins, making funny noises and pulling silly faces at them. They both giggled at her.

'Mum, can I go ice-skating this half-term holiday?' Emily asked hopefully. She didn't get to ice-skate regularly because it was too expensive, but her mum knew how much she loved it and tried to take her at least once every holiday.

'Not this time, Em. I've got no one to

look after the twins while your dad's away with work,' Mrs Walker said. 'I promise we can go at Easter though.'

'But that's two months away,' Emily protested.

Mrs Walker's voice softened. 'I'm really sorry, Em. It's just not possible this holiday.'

Emily sighed and tried not to mind too much. She knew her mum was really busy and tired, and that she would have taken her if she could. 'OK,' she muttered and shut her blue eyes for a moment, letting herself imagine that she was whizzing across the ice. She could skate quite fast now and longed to be able to go more often.

Emily could remember the very first time she had been skating at one of her friend's birthday parties. When she had got on the ice, she had skated slowly round the rink the first time, but then had just let go of the barrier. She'd begun to go faster and faster and, before she knew it, had gone all the way round without stopping. None of the others had been able to skate straight away like that and the skating teacher had told her that she could be very good if she skated regularly. Emily could still remember how proud she'd felt.

Splodge!

A dollop of food landed on her arm. She opened her eyes quickly. Rose had grabbed the bowl and plunged both fists into it. She was waving them around, sending baby food flying. Jasmine chortled.

Emily giggled too and quickly grabbed

the kitchen roll so she could wipe up the mess before her mum noticed.

After the twins had finished eating, Mrs Walker took them upstairs and Emily went outside into the garden. It was a cold, crisp February day. She ran forward and jumped into the air, crossing her arms over her chest and spinning round as she did so. She landed, arms

out, imagining ice under her feet, not grass. If only she really was skating! Emily imagined it with all her heart as she began to pretend to do an ice-skating spin, turning once, twice . . .

She gasped. She was spinning round a third time and a fourth, getting faster and faster! Suddenly Emily was twirling in a blur of silver light. In the blink of an eye, she felt things change. Her jeans turned to tights and her feet suddenly felt heavy. *I've got ice skates on!* she realized. As the thought flashed across her mind, the glittering light began to clear. Emily was still spinning, but began slowing to a stop. She looked round in astonishment.

She was standing in the middle of a frozen lake!

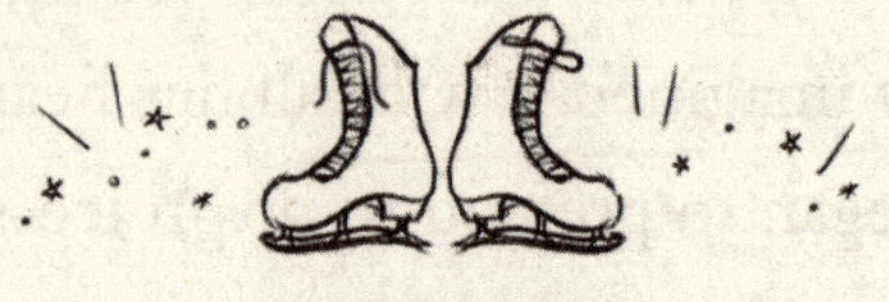

Chapter Two
Magic!

Everywhere Emily looked was white and sparkling. Long icicles hung from the branches of trees. The sun shone down, but there seemed to be little heat in its rays. She shut her eyes then opened them again quickly. She was still standing on a frozen lake!

I must be dreaming! she thought in astonishment. *But how can I be?*

She looked down. She was wearing white boots and a short sunshine-yellow skating dress.

'Ah, Emily, there you are!' a voice behind her called.

Emily was so surprised she jumped. Immediately her skates slipped from underneath her and she fell over. She gasped as she bumped down. The ice was hard and cold. If it was a dream, it was the most realistic one she'd ever had!

A tall, slim woman with dark hair tied back in a bun and a knee-length maroon dress was skating over the lake towards her. She looked normal – well, apart from her ears, which were long and pointed.

'Well, well, you must be Emily Walker. Welcome to the Land of Ice and Winter.' The woman with the strange ears stopped in front of Emily and reached out her hand. 'Up you get, child,' she said briskly. 'Don't just sit there.'

Emily stood up in a daze. 'Who are you?'

'My name is Madame Letsworth. I am an ice sylph and the headteacher here at the Magic Ice-skating Academy. I've been waiting for you. You're the last one to arrive.'

'Magic Ice-skating Academy?' Emily echoed. 'I . . . I don't understand.'

'It will all be explained when we get to the school.' Madame Letsworth turned and skated back the way she had come. 'Come along, child. Don't dawdle!'

Emily hesitated. But she didn't want to be left alone so she hurriedly followed the teacher. As they skated round a bend, Emily's eyes widened as she saw an enormous building in front of them. It was a mansion built of grey stone with a set of wide stone steps leading up to a big door. But instead of having a drive running up to it, as a house would normally have, the frozen lake went all the way to the steps just as if it was a road.

Madame Letsworth skated to the steps and took two pairs of skate guards –

covers that go over the bottom of skates – from a box at the side of the steps. She handed one pair to Emily.

'Put these on until we get inside and then you can take your skates off.'

Emily did as she was told. Madame Letsworth went to the top of the steps and opened the door. A wave of warm air billowed out and Emily heard the sound of chattering voices. She went up the

steps. Inside there was a large entrance hall painted a rich, deep-red colour with a dark wooden floor. A fire was burning in a large fireplace. Several adults who had pointed ears like Madame Letsworth's were carrying silver trays around, and on the trays were mugs of steaming hot chocolate and plates of biscuits. They were handing them out to a group of about fourteen girls. Some of the girls were tall and others small; their hair and skin colour were different, but they were all about ten years old and wearing ice-skating dresses, just like Emily, with matching fleecy slipper-boots.

Madame Letsworth turned to Emily. 'Welcome to the Magic Ice-skating Academy!' she said with a smile.

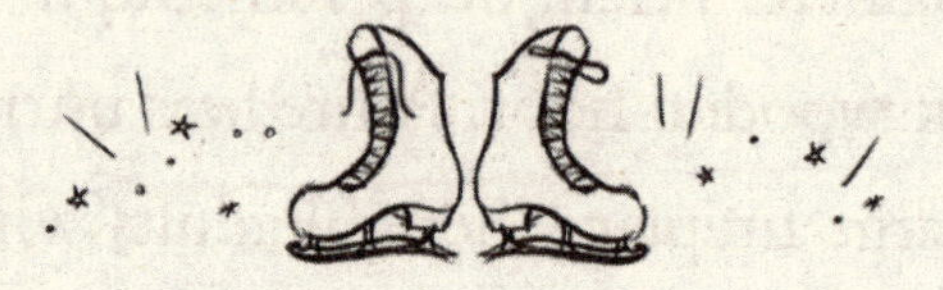

Chapter Three
Skating School

Madame Letsworth led Emily over to a row of lockers at the side of the room. They each had names written on: *Molly Wang*; *Hannah Peters*; *Camilla Meredith*; *Amanda Duval*; *Alice Jenson*; *Tilda Obigiu* . . .

Emily unlaced her skates and put on the pair of yellow slipper-boots that were in the locker with her name on. A hundred questions were whizzing through her mind. She caught sight of a girl with waist-length straight dark hair, pale skin and very light-blue eyes who was wearing a red ice-skating dress. 'Miss,' the girl said, coming over to Madame Letsworth. 'The girl with the black hair over there took three biscuits. I saw her.' She pointed across the room.

'That's all right, Amanda. Don't worry about it. There are more biscuits in the kitchen,' Madame Letsworth said briskly.

The girl looked a bit disappointed that no one was going to be told off. 'Oh. It's just I thought you should know, Miss.' She moved closer to Madame Letsworth. 'It's really very scary not knowing anyone here. Can I stay with you?' she said, blinking up at the teacher.

A tall girl with strawberry-blonde hair and a deep-green skating dress who was standing nearby caught Emily's eye. 'Oh, *puh-lease*!' she mouthed, glancing at the dark-haired girl. Emily grinned. The dark-haired girl *had* sounded a bit annoying.

As Amanda left, trailing behind Madame Letsworth, the tall girl came up to Emily. 'Did you hear that?' She imitated Amanda's slightly whiny voice. '*It's really very scary. Can I stay with you?*'

Emily giggled. 'Hi, I'm Emily.'

'I'm Camilla,' the girl said. 'This place is cool, isn't it? Did you know the teachers are ice sylphs? That's why they've got pointed ears. The teacher who brought me here told me that there aren't any humans in this land – well,

apart from us. We've been brought here by magic for a special reason.'

'Why?' Emily knew she should probably feel scared, but she was just excited and curious. Deep down, she somehow felt that nothing bad would happen in this strange magic land.

'She wouldn't tell me.' Camilla nudged her. 'It looks like we're about to find out though.'

Madame Letsworth was clapping her

hands. 'Right, girls. Now you have all arrived, why don't you come to the school hall and I will explain why you are here.'

She led the way down a corridor and into a big hall with two rows of chairs. Emily sat down next to a girl with a mischievous grin and straight black hair that fell to just above her shoulders. 'Hi,' she whispered to Emily. 'I'm Molly Wang.'

'I'm Emily Walker,' Emily whispered back as Camilla sat down on the other side of her.

Madame Letsworth began to speak again. Emily turned all her attention to her, hoping to find out what was going on.

The headteacher smiled round at all

the girls. 'I would like to welcome you all to the Land of Ice and Winter. We who live here are not human. We are ice sylphs. We have brought you here by magic because we need a human girl to help us. We have a problem in our land and only a human girl with ice-skating deep in her heart can perform the task that will solve it. The person who is chosen will be crowned our Ice Princess and will have her heart's desire granted.'

Molly raised her hand. 'What will she have to do?'

'You will find that out in time,' replied Madame Letsworth. 'But first you must decide if you wish to stay here at our Ice-skating Academy. If you do, you will spend your days taking lessons with skating coaches and having other classes that will improve your skating, such as gymnastics and ballet. You will learn all about this land and the magic in it. And you will also take part in skating competitions where each week the winner will be awarded a different coloured pair of ice-skating boots. These competitions will help us choose our Ice Princess at the end of six weeks.'

An excited buzz of whispering rose.

Madame Letsworth allowed just the briefest of interruptions before continuing. 'No time will pass in the human world while you are here, no one will miss you, and when you eventually return, it will be as if you had never left. Only you will know where you have been.' She looked around at the girls. 'It is up to you now: will you stay here or will you choose to go home? Each girl must make that decision for herself.'

'Oh, wow!' Molly whispered to Emily, looking as if she was about to burst with delight. 'I am *so* not going home!'

Emily knew just how she felt. She'd miss home, but if no one there would miss her then she knew she would stay. It would be like a dream come true to live in a magic land, skating every day! She turned to Camilla, her eyes shining. 'I'm going to stay! Are you?'

'Definitely!' declared Camilla. All around them people were saying the same thing. Apart from one girl with red hair.

She stood up. 'I . . . I want to go home,' she stammered.

Emily could hardly believe it.

But Madame Letsworth just nodded. 'Very well,' she said. 'You are right to say so if you do not wish to stay, Eleanore. Come here.'

The girl approached her nervously.

The others watched as the teacher said something to her. The girl nodded and relaxed. Madame Letsworth touched a hand to her head.

The girl started to turn round. Emily's eyes widened as she spun faster and faster

and then suddenly disappeared in a cloud of silver light.

'She's gone!' Molly gasped.

'Eleanore has returned home,' Madame Letsworth told everyone in the hall. 'She will not remember her visit here except as a vague dream that makes her smile. Would anyone else like to return home?'

The other girls quickly shook their heads.

'Well, remember that you can always return if you wish, but also bear in mind –' Madame Letsworth's voice took on a note of warning – 'that we can always send you back if you prove to be an unsuitable student. I will be your headteacher and one of the skating coaches, but you will be taught by other teachers as well. You will meet them later, but first let us go to the ice-skating rink.'

As everyone stood up, Emily looked round. There were fourteen girls left now. At the end of six weeks, one of them would get to be the Ice Princess, help the land and have her heart's desire.

Oh, wow, thought Emily. *I hope it's me!*

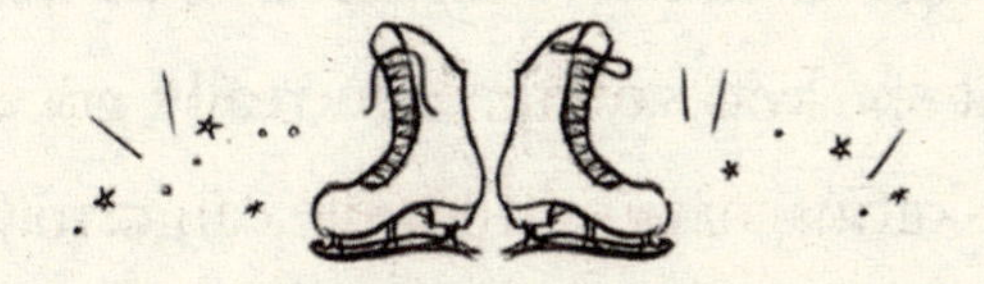

Chapter Four
On the Ice

The girls fetched their ice-skating boots from the entrance and followed Madame Letsworth out of the hall. Emily had so many questions buzzing through her mind. She wanted to know more about the lessons and where they would sleep and what the Ice Princess was going to have to do.

Amanda, the girl with the long dark

hair, was glued to Madame Letsworth's side again. Emily could hear snatches of what she was saying: 'I'm really good at ice-skating,' she said loudly. 'I go to lessons three times a week and Mummy says I'm going to be an Olympic champion one day . . .'

Emily couldn't believe she was being quite so boastful.

Madame Letsworth sighed. 'Why don't you go and talk to some of the others, Amanda?'

'Oh, no, I'm *much* happier talking to you,' said Amanda sweetly, taking hold of the headteacher's hand.

They reached large double doors at the end of the corridor. Madame Letsworth opened them and all the girls gasped. A massive ice rink lay in front of them.

There were seats all round it and it was covered by a glass dome. They could see the sky and clouds and pale sun through the glass. Little white dots were dancing over the surface of the ice. As Emily looked closely, she realized that they were alive. 'What are they?' she burst out.

'Frost fairies,' answered Madame Letsworth. 'They fly above the ice all

over this land. They smooth it so that it is perfect for skating.'

One of the white dots danced off the ice and swooped up in front of them. Emily saw that it really was a little fairy, about two centimetres high, with pale-blonde hair, light-blue eyes and gauzy wings.

'We only have machines to smooth the ice at home,' said Molly, her eyes wide as she watched the little creature dart away. 'I wish we had fairies!'

Madame Letsworth chuckled. 'Oh, I'm sure you'll find quite a few differences between the human world and this world, but one thing's the same, and that is the skating. I am sure you are all longing to get on to the ice!'

Five minutes later, and after a flurry of lacing boots, the girls all headed to the rink entrance. Emily skated off as soon as she got on to the ice and then stopped as she suddenly realized that most of the other girls were doing warm-up exercises: stretching their legs, bending their knees, skating low to the ice in a sitting position.

Madame Letsworth saw her face. 'You haven't had lessons before, have you, Emily?'

Emily shook her head.

'It's always important to start by warming up. You'll learn about that in class this afternoon. For now, just copy some of the others.'

As Emily bent and stretched her legs, Camilla came over to her. 'So, you don't have skating lessons?' she said curiously.

Emily shook her head. 'No, I go

dancing every week, but I don't have skating lessons. Do you?'

'Oh, yes, I go ice-skating five times a week,' Camilla said. 'I compete loads too.'

'Like Hannah,' commented Molly, who was standing nearby. She pointed to a slim girl with a blue dress, blonde ponytail and large blue eyes. 'I was talking to her earlier.'

'I know her from back home. We've skated against each other in competitions,' said Camilla. Her mouth hardened as she glanced at the blonde girl, who had now gone on to the ice and was skating smoothly backwards in decreasing circles. 'I usually beat her though.'

'That's not what Hannah said,' Molly muttered to Emily as Camilla stepped on to the ice and skated off, doing a showy set of forward and backward crossover steps. Molly grinned at Emily. 'Well, catch you later!'

She set off at top speed across the ice.

Emily followed her more cautiously. She skated round the outside of the rink. It was so interesting watching the others that she was happy just skating round, practising gliding on one leg for as long as she could before changing to the other leg. She watched Hannah, the girl Molly had pointed out, doing graceful spirals, one leg lifted high in the air, Camilla turning into a fast layback spin and Molly trying to do a difficult jump called a double flip.

Maybe I'll learn to skate like that too, thought Emily excitedly.

★

After forty minutes, Madame Letsworth called them all off the ice and they went to see the rest of the school – the classroom where they would go for some lessons, the common room where they could relax, the music room, the library and finally the dorms where they would be sleeping.

There were two dorms on the first floor called Ice Owls and Snow Foxes, and one on the floor above called Frost Fairies. Madame Letsworth read out a list of names. 'In the Ice Owls dorm there will be Amanda, Zoe, Heather, Tasha and Olivia; in the Snow Foxes, Camilla, Tess, Clare, Helena and Emily; and the remaining four of you are in Frost Fairies,' the teacher said. 'That's Molly, Hannah, Tilda and Alice. There will be a spare bed in your dorm, Frost Fairies.'

They all hurried to see where they would be sleeping. The dorms were large rooms with beds lined up against one wall, facing the door. Big windows behind them let in lots of light. The beds were covered with colourful patchwork quilts. At the end of each bed was a name tag, and opposite each of them was a wardrobe with an in-built dressing table and chest of drawers.

Emily was in the bed nearest the door in her dorm. In her wardrobe there were two more ice-skating dresses, a thick fake-fur coat, two pairs of jeans, tracksuit bottoms, waterproof padded trousers and a number of different tops. In the drawers were underwear, tights, socks, a ballet leotard and ballet shoes, a gymnastics leotard, gloves, a scarf and leg warmers. Everything she could possibly need!

Camilla threw herself down on her bed and looked around. 'So, this is our dorm. It's a bit dullsville, isn't it? No TV or PS3. Not even a CD player!'

Tess was in the bed next to Camilla. 'Yeah. I've got all of them in my bedroom at home.'

'Me too,' said Camilla.

Emily didn't say anything. She had a CD player in her room at home, but that was all. She looked round at the others, all nodding in agreement with Camilla. She usually made friends easily, but she felt a bit shy around these girls. They all seemed so cool and confident.

'Hey, look! There's a timetable on the door!' said Clare. They all crowded round.

Emily read and re-read it. All the lessons sounded brilliant! It wasn't just skating lessons – every day was packed with a mixture of skating, gymnastics, cross-country skiing, music and learning about the land. Emily was delighted to see that there were ballet lessons too. Everything sounded such good fun!

Camilla didn't seem to think so. 'Some of the lessons sound *so* boring. I mean, the skating will be great, but who wants to learn about this land?'

Emily kept quiet. She did!

'Not me.' Tess sat back on her bed. 'So, what do you think of all the others here?'

'Well, that Amanda is totally annoying, isn't she?' said Camilla. 'And as for Hannah! Doesn't that girl ever crack a smile? She's like that back in the real world too. Miss I'm-so-serious-and-think-I'm-such-an-awesome-skater.' She looked round with satisfaction. 'We've definitely got the best dorm.' She put up her hand in a high five. 'Snow Foxes rule OK!'

The others all slapped hands with her. Emily hesitated, but Camilla looked at her sharply and she hastily joined in.

Lunch was served in the hall. There were jacket potatoes with different fillings and salads, and for pudding lots of different flavours of ice cream. Frost fairies fluttered around, clearing up any spills and carrying jugs of orange juice around in teams, twenty little fairies per jug. They poured the juice out, chattering in high-pitched voices that Emily couldn't understand. She said thank you. Two of the fairies landed on her hands and looked at her curiously, their wings fluttering. Emily smiled at them and they grinned back before flying away.

After they had finished their lunch, Madame Letsworth and the other two skating teachers came to meet them. Madame Letsworth explained that the girls would be taught in three groups – beginners, intermediate and advanced. She would be teaching the advanced group, which included Hannah, Camilla,

Zoe, Amanda and Molly; Monsieur Carvallio, a tall, dark-skinned ice sylph, was going to be coaching the beginners' group, which included Emily, Heather and Tilda. All the other girls were in the intermediate group with another of the teachers, Madame Li.

'You are all at different ability levels

right now,' Madame Letsworth explained. 'But there is one thing you all have in common and that is talent. Hopefully you will use your time here to develop that talent. You may use the rink any time you are free.'

Emily hugged herself. She couldn't wait!

'But now let me tell you more about the weekly competitions,' Madame Letsworth went on, looking serious. 'This week, you will need to skate a two-minute programme to music. It won't be judged so much on technical ability as on your ability to express feeling on the ice. The winner will be the girl whose programme most makes us believe she is dancing with her whole heart.'

'And is the prize going to be ice skates?' Camilla asked eagerly.

'Yes. The winner of this week's competition will be presented with a pair of white skates with silver laces and, as it is your first competition, she will also be able to ask for one thing as the prize,' Madame Letsworth said. 'If the school can provide it, it will be granted.'

Hannah put up her hand. 'What about music?'

'You will find music boxes both in the music room and here, by the ice,' Madame Letsworth said. 'You must choose a piece of music from them to skate to, plan your routine and at the end of the week you will perform it for the judges and your fellow students. Now, you have half an hour and then it is time for your first ice-skating lesson. Please be on the ice by two o'clock.'

She and the other teachers left the room. Immediately the noise level rose.

'Cool!' said Camilla. 'I like competitions.'

Emily felt rather daunted. 'I've never done one before.'

Clare turned to Camilla. 'I bet you'll win. I was watching you skating before. You're the best here. I bet you'll even be chosen to be the Ice Princess.'

Camilla smiled. 'Thanks. I know Madame Letsworth did say technical ability wouldn't count so much in the competition this week, but then if you can't ice-skate very well, you're not going to be able to express yourself, are you?'

Amanda heard and came over. 'We're

both going to be in the advanced group so we'll be able to help each other, Camilla. I know you're not quite as good as me, but I'm sure you'll soon catch up.'

Camilla's eyebrows rose up to her hair.

'Well, I'm going to go and listen to some music,' said Amanda. 'See you in class later! Byeee!' She waved at Camilla as if they were best friends and hurried away.

Camilla looked outraged. 'Does annoying Amanda really think that she's better than me?'

'You're loads better than she is, Camilla!' said Tess, shaking her head.

Emily let their voices fade out and thought about the competition. She had watched loads of ice-skating on TV back at home, but she had never done a

routine before. She felt really excited at the thought of planning it. *I'm going to practise really hard and then maybe I'll be able to do some jumps and spins properly by the end of the week*, she thought. She imagined herself taking off and turning a perfect jump while everyone watched. Wouldn't it be wonderful if she could do that?

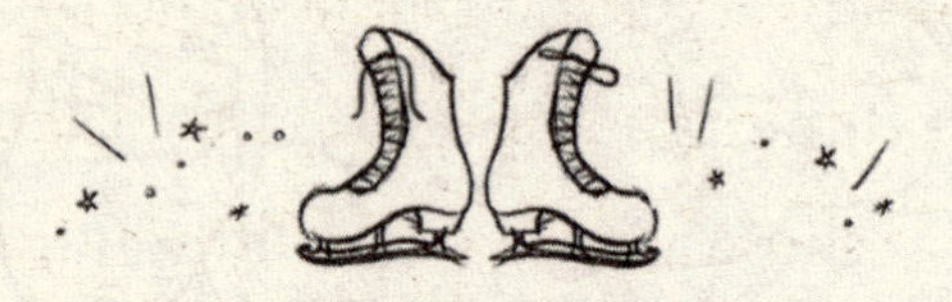

Chapter Five

Making Friends

When Emily started her first ice-skating lesson, she realized that although she was very good at dancing, she had done less ice-skating than anyone else in the school. Even the other two beginners, Tilda and Heather, were better than her. But it was lovely to be skating and she tried as hard as she could. Monsieur Carvallio taught her how to go forwards and backwards and do different turns. She had very good balance and soon picked things up. By the end of the lesson she was able to do little jumps above the ice in a move Monsieur Carvallio said was called a bunnyhop, and was trying out a simple turning jump called a three jump. 'Well done,' Monsieur Carvallio said, smiling at her. 'You have really improved in just one lesson, Emily.'

'Not like me!' sighed Tilda. 'I fell over about a hundred times!'

'You need to learn to slow down and think, Tilda,' Monsieur Carvallio told her. 'But you have great gymnastic ability. You'll be a really good skater one day. Now let us try that two-foot spin again.'

Every so often, Emily would glance

round the rink at the other groups. Amanda was clearly good at doing spins, but she did move her arms and hands in a really fussy way. She seemed keen to try and catch Madame Letsworth's eyes with every movement. Emily thought Hannah and Camilla, who both seemed to do much less, looked much more elegant. Hannah's skating was very crisp and precise, and, because she was tall and slim, she looked very graceful on the ice. Camilla looked incredibly confident and cool; she skated around as if she owned the rink. Molly had loads of energy on the ice and fell over a lot, but she never seemed to care. She just scrambled up and tried again!

After their lesson, they were allowed to free-skate. Molly skated up to Emily at breakneck speed. 'Hi there!' she said,

skidding to a halt and sending ice crystals spraying up around her. 'Do you want to come and skate with Hannah and me? We're going to play some games.'

Emily nodded eagerly and followed her over to Hannah. At first, she felt a bit nervous because Hannah was such a good skater, but the blonde girl smiled at her in a friendly way. 'Hi, Emily. I saw you starting to do three jumps. You were doing them really well.'

'Thanks. I've never done any jumps before ever. Actually, I've never even had a lesson before,' Emily admitted.

'Then you were doing brilliantly!' Hannah enthused. 'You must be really talented. It took me loads of lessons to get on to doing jumps.'

Emily glowed with pleasure.

'Let's play a game,' said Molly, skating in circles. 'How about follow-my-leader? Come on!'

They set off. Emily and Hannah were fairly sensible when they were the leader, but Molly made them do all sorts of silly things – skating backwards looking through their legs, pretending to be an elephant, and then flapping their arms, quacking and waddling on the ice as if they were ducks.

'You have to quack!' she kept insisting when Emily and Hannah didn't.

'I can't,' said Hannah, looking a bit embarrassed.

'You have to. Come on! Like this! Quack quack! Quack quack!' Molly made a silly quacking sound and waggled her bottom.

Hannah and Emily looked at each other and then giggled and copied her. Emily saw Amanda give them an astonished look from the side and almost fall over in shock.

'I love ice-skating school!' she said happily.

'Me too!' Molly declared.

Hannah nodded. 'Have you thought

about your routine for the competition at the end of the week, Emily?' she asked as they came off the ice.

'No, not really,' admitted Emily. 'I don't actually know where to start.'

'We're going to go to the music room at break time tomorrow to choose some music. Do you want to come with us?' Molly asked.

'Definitely!' Emily replied.

'Emily!' Camilla's sharp voice cut through the air. She was standing by the lockers with Tess, Clare and Helena. 'We're all going up to the dorm now. Come on!'

Emily wanted to stay with Hannah and Molly, but she thought she'd better go with her dorm-mates, so she said goodbye and quickly changed out of her boots and followed the rest of the Snow Foxes upstairs. They were all talking about their lives back home, the bands they were into and the things they liked to do when they weren't ice-skating, which seemed to be mainly shopping and listening to music. Emily couldn't help wishing she was still with Molly and Hannah. They seemed much more fun!

★

The rest of the day passed by in a whirl. The girls had a cross-country skiing lesson after their afternoon break and then after supper Emily explored the grounds with the other Snow Foxes. There were bubbling hot springs where the girls could go and swim, frozen rivers where they could skate, a sledging slope and woods where Emily was sure she glimpsed some white fluffy fox cubs, and kennels where lots of big silver-grey husky dogs were kept for pulling sledges. Emily thought it was all amazing.

By the time she fell into bed that night she didn't think she'd ever felt so tired. Her muscles ached from all the skating and her head was spinning. She almost didn't want to go to sleep in case she woke up and found it had all been a dream. *But it isn't*, she thought in delight as she snuggled down under her patchwork quilt. *It's real!* She wondered what was happening at home and then remembered what Madame Letsworth had said. No time would be passing so everything would be exactly the same as when she had left. Her mum would be in the house settling the twins. No one would be missing her at all.

It was a weird thought, but also strangely comforting. Emily's real life was waiting for her back at home, but, right now, she was here in the magic Land of Ice and Winter and she was determined to enjoy every moment!

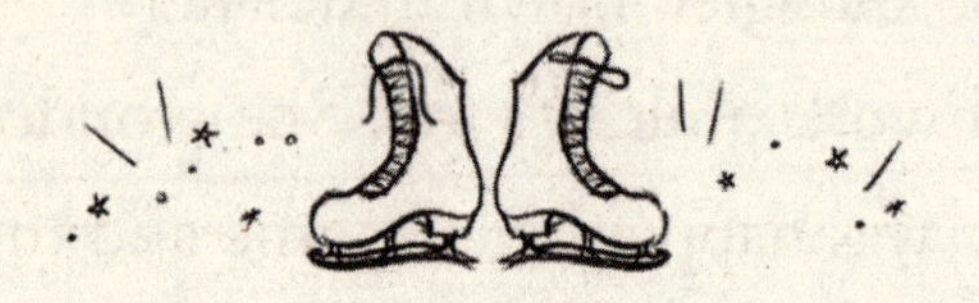

Chapter Six

Molly and Hannah

The next day started with a ballet class. Molly and Hannah greeted Emily in the changing room and made space beside them so she could get changed into her blue leotard. 'Did you sleep OK?' Molly asked.

Emily nodded. 'Really well. How about you?'

'We talked for ages. Madame

Letsworth came in three times and started to get really cross,' said Hannah.

'Tilda and Alice in our dorm are really good fun,' said Molly. 'Tilda's brilliant at gymnastics – she can do six cartwheels in a row. We all tried, but none of us could do more than three. I crashed into the bin and it ended up on my foot!'

Emily giggled and wished she was in the Frost Fairies dorm. It sounded fun!

The ballet teacher, Madame Breshnev, called them into class. Because of the dance lessons she'd had back home, Emily could easily do the things that most of the others found hard – hold an arabesque without wobbling, stretch her leg out to one side, turn a pirouette. Madame Breshnev was clearly delighted with her and got her to demonstrate several times. But when Emily danced a sequence of steps at the end of the class and Madame Breshnev told her she was excellent, Camilla scowled. 'Do you think you could show off any more?' she whispered unkindly as Emily went back to join the others by the barre.

Emily felt hurt, but luckily Hannah and Molly were nearby and so she stayed with them for the rest of the lesson.

After ballet, they went to the music room to choose some music for their routine. Emily was surprised to see that there wasn't a normal CD player there. Instead there was a large purple box with a lid on and silver buttons shaped like stars arranged in columns all over the front. At the top of each column there

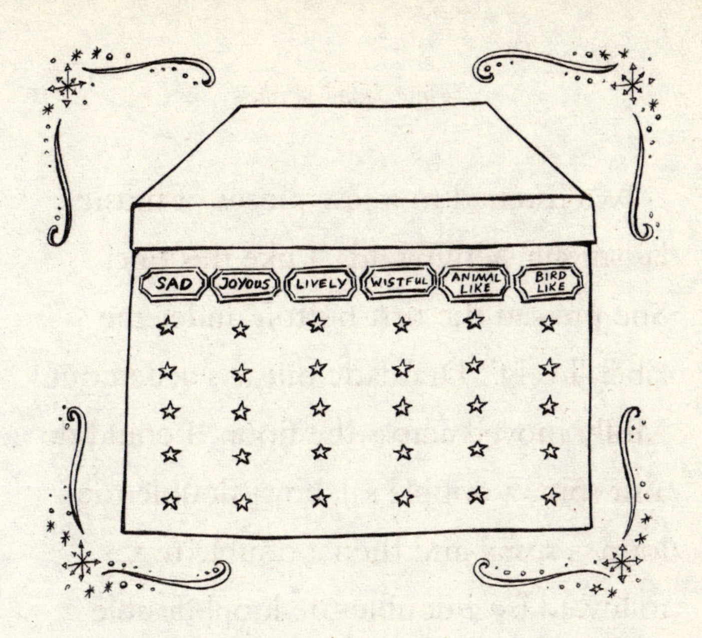

was a label: 'sad'; 'joyous'; 'lively'; 'wistful'; 'animal-like'; 'bird-like'.

'How does it work?' Emily wondered, examining the box.

'Molly and I came yesterday evening,' Hannah said. 'You just press the buttons to hear different pieces of music using the labels as a guide for the type of music you want. When you find some music you like, you press the same button on the box at the rink and that piece of music plays.'

'We listened to a few pieces of music last night,' Molly said. 'I like this one.' She pressed the first button under the label 'lively'. Dramatic music swelled out. Molly moved across the floor. 'I could do a sit spin, a double salchow–double toe loop, a spiral and then a double flip, followed by a double toe loop–double loop and finish with a layback spin.'

'That would be quite hard,' said Hannah cautiously.

'I know, but imagine if I got it right,' said Molly. 'It would be awesome! Let's find you a piece of music too, Emily.'

'I was wondering if I could use one of the dances I've done in ballet,' Emily said, 'but turn it into an ice-skating routine instead.' She had been thinking about a dance she had done where she had been a bluebird. She started pressing the buttons to try and find a piece of music that might work. The first few pieces of music weren't right, but then she heard one that just might do. She began to dance to it – stepping into an arabesque, sweeping her arms round, dancing forward and then jumping high into the air and landing lightly, perfectly in time. She danced her way through the whole

dance, adapting it to the music as she went. When she finished, she saw the other two staring at her.

'Wow!' breathed Molly. 'I saw how good you were in ballet class, but when you're dancing properly like that, you're brilliant!'

Hannah nodded. 'That was great, Emily!'

Emily blushed modestly. 'It wasn't that good.'

But her friends ignored her. 'If you get a bit better at skating and then skate as you dance, you'll be amazing,' said Molly. 'Your balance is so good and you're so flexible.'

'You should pick up doing spirals really quickly,' Hannah told her. 'They're just arabesques, but moving on the ice. Actually, you could easily add some jumps and spins. If you want, why don't you put the music on and show me the dance again and I'll tell you how.'

'I *do* want!' Emily said eagerly.

And so, for the next twenty minutes, Hannah and Molly went through the music, telling Emily what she should try and where to do it. 'If you can't manage the difficult moves by the end of the week, you can always make the routine easier,' Hannah said.

Emily nodded, but she was determined to practise as hard as she could and do as good a routine as possible.

Molly looked at the music box. 'It's amazing how this thing works just by pressing the buttons, isn't it?' she said. 'I guess there must be CDs or something inside it.'

She lifted the lid and immediately gasped, dropping the lid in surprise.

'What is it?' Emily demanded. 'What's in there?'

Molly pointed at the box, her eyes wide. 'It's . . . it's not CDs!' she stammered.

Emily cautiously opened the lid with Hannah peering over her shoulder. Inside the box, there were lots of levers, spinning discs and wheels – and four small, silvery-blue dragons to work them! Both girls gasped. Each dragon was about the size of one of their hands. They looked up at the girls and made a friendly chirruping throaty noise.

'Little dragons make it work!' breathed Emily. 'Oh, wow!'

'I can't believe this!' said Hannah. They all looked at each other and then

giggled at the strangeness of it all. 'It's so weird.'

'But amazingly brilliant!' said Molly in delight. 'I love this land!'

One of the dragons waved his front legs at them as if asking for the lid to be shut. Emily carefully closed it. 'Sorry to disturb you,' she said, and the dragon chirruped at her in reply.

Just then, the bell went. The girls hurried back to their dorms to get their clothes for skating.

The other Snow Foxes were all talking together as Emily walked into their dorm.

'It'll be so much fun!' Camilla was saying. As Emily came in, she looked round. 'Where have you been, Emily? We've been planning this great trick on Amanda. I'm going to make her look really silly in the competition.'

Emily wondered what the trick was. She liked jokes, but she hoped it wasn't too mean. 'I've just been in the music room with Molly and Hannah,' Emily said. She longed to tell them all about the dragons in the music box, but for a moment she wondered if they would think it babyish to be so excited about the little creatures.

Camilla raised her eyebrows. 'Oh, I see.'

Emily could tell that Camilla wasn't

pleased. 'We . . . we were just listening to music,' she said.

Camilla looked at her coldly. 'Well, if you want to hang around with the Frost Fairies dorm instead of us then that's up to you. But, you know something, Emily? You can't hang around with them *and* us. If you want to be friends with them then none of us are going to talk to you.'

Emily stared. Camilla couldn't be serious! But, to her astonishment, she saw that the others in the dorm were either nodding or just looking away from Emily.

Camilla turned back to the others. 'OK, so we've got our plan. You watch and see what I do! Come on, let's go down to the rink and see if Amanda's there.' And with that, she hurried out of the dorm with the other girls following behind.

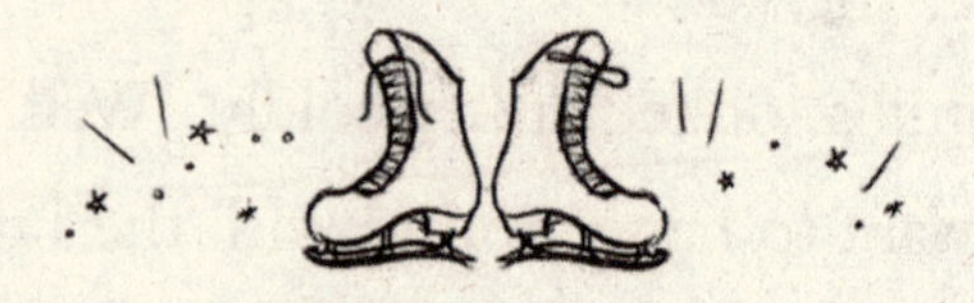

Chapter Seven
Friends or Not?

Emily felt sick as she got changed. What was she going to do? She wanted to be friends with Molly and Hannah, but she didn't want Camilla and the other Snow Foxes ignoring her. *How can I choose?* she thought anxiously. *That's horrible.*

She went down to the rink. Camilla was skating with Amanda. Emily remembered what Camilla had said about

the trick she was going to play. Should she say something? Neither Molly nor Hannah was at the rink yet, so Emily put her skates on and started to warm up.

'That looks awesome!' Camilla was saying as Amanda did a strange move with her arms, wafting them from side to side in a very dramatic way.

Amanda looked very pleased. 'I'm being Juliet longing for her Romeo,' she said, sweeping back her long hair. 'My mum always says it's my best routine.'

'Oh, it's brilliant, Amanda,' said Camilla, a wicked glint in her eyes. 'Only maybe you could do with even more expression.'

Emily stared. Amanda was being extremely dramatic already. She didn't need more expression!

'*More* expression?' Amanda said in surprise.

Camilla opened her eyes wide and nodded. '*Definitely!*'

Amanda performed her routine again, this time clasping her hands to her chest and throwing back her head. Camilla stifled a grin. 'Oh, yes, that's perfect!' she said, skating up to Amanda. 'Tell you what, why don't I help you with your routine for the competition?'

Amanda smiled at her. 'That would be great. Thanks!'

Emily saw Tess, Clare and Helena giggling at the side of the rink and she suddenly twigged. Camilla had obviously decided to encourage Amanda's dramatic gestures to make her look really silly. Emily felt uncomfortable about it. Amanda was annoying, but it was horrible of Camilla to pretend to be Amanda's friend while really laughing at her behind her back and trying to make her look stupid.

Emily skated off, not wanting to be part of it. As she went round, she tried to remember the routine Hannah and Molly had suggested. She talked to herself as she skated. 'Crossover steps here and then a three jump and a spiral.' She began to practise. She wobbled a few times when she started doing the routine, but soon began to get the hang of it, gliding on one foot across the ice. Encouraged, she did a three turn, turning from forwards to backwards and then jumping a single toe loop, something that she had watched the

intermediate skaters doing. She landed on two feet, but she didn't fall over and felt very pleased with herself. Maybe she would be good enough to put it into her routine by the end of the week.

'What are you doing?' Camilla demanded, leaving Amanda and skating up to Emily.

'Just practising bits for the competition,' she replied.

'Well, I think you want to keep it as easy as possible,' Camilla said bossily. 'No spins and spirals and definitely no proper jumps like a toe loop. You're not ready for them.'

'I thought that if I practise all week, I might be,' said Emily hopefully.

Camilla shook her head. 'You'll just look stupid. You'll fall down in front of everyone and come last. You'll be much better off doing something really, really simple.'

Hannah skated up behind her. 'That's rubbish, Camilla!' she said. 'Emily's still got five days to practise. She might not have got everything right yet, but it's a great routine.' She turned to Emily. 'Don't listen to her, Emily. You were doing really well. She's just worried you're going to beat her.'

'Emily? Beat me? I don't think so,' Camilla snorted. 'Anyway, who asked you to interfere, Hannah Peters?'

'I'm not interfering. I'm Emily's friend,' said Hannah, meeting Camilla's glare.

'Oh, are you?' Camilla said, looking challengingly at Emily.

Emily went red, not knowing what to

say. Just then, to her absolute relief, there was the loud blast of a whistle and the teachers skated on to the ice.

'Come on, girls. Time to begin!' Madame Letsworth called. Emily skated away as fast as she could.

Emily forced all her problems out of her mind during the lesson, trying to concentrate on her skating and nothing else. But as soon as the lesson was over, she left the ice and headed straight to the hall, away from all the others. Emily didn't know what to do. Questions ran through her mind. Would Camilla really not talk to her if she was friends with Hannah and Molly? And what should she do about her routine? Was she going to do the easy routine or the hard one?

I don't want to look stupid like Camilla said, she thought. *Maybe I should just do the easy routine.*

She had just reached the hall when Molly and Hannah came running up behind her.

'Hey, Em, how come you dashed off so quickly?' Molly said.

'Are you OK?' Hannah asked, searching Emily's face.

Emily tried to nod, but as she tried to smile, her face crumpled and she had to bite her lip to stop herself from crying.

'You're not OK.' Molly frowned. 'Oh, Em, Hannah told me what Camilla said about not doing anything difficult in your routine. Is that what's upsetting you? You're not going to listen to her, are you? She's just scared you're going to

skate better than her and win.'

'It's not that,' Emily said unhappily.

'What is it then?' asked Hannah in concern.

Emily saw the worry on Hannah and Molly's faces and suddenly it all burst out. 'Camilla's said that none of the Snow Foxes will talk to me if I go round with you two.'

'How dare she!' exclaimed Molly.

'Oh, Emily. What are you going to

do?' Hannah asked in concern.

Emily didn't say anything.

'You are going to be friends with us, aren't you?' Molly said.

Looking from Molly's upset face to Hannah's anxious one, Emily knew the answer. 'Yes, of course I am,' she said. She couldn't *not* be friends with them. They were much nicer than all the Snow Foxes.

Molly grinned. 'Phew!'

Hannah still looked worried. 'It won't be easy for you though, if the rest of your dorm aren't talking to you.'

Emily realized she was right. 'No,' she said slowly. 'It won't.'

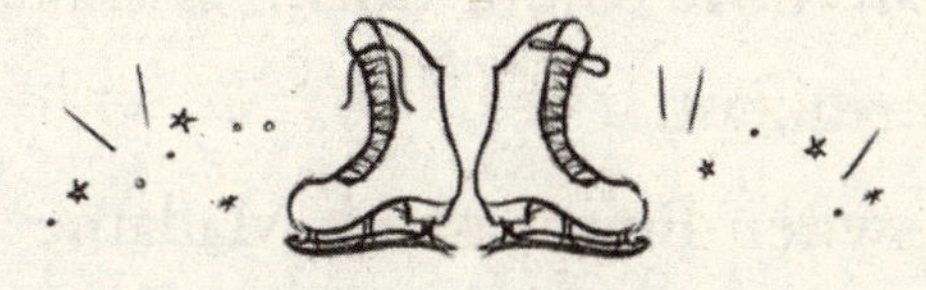

Chapter Eight
Which Routine?

Emily sat with Hannah and Molly at lunchtime and Camilla looked very cross. After that, none of the Snow Foxes talked to Emily for the rest of the day. *They'll stop it soon*, Emily thought. However, the next morning, they continued to ignore her, talking to each other, but pretending they hadn't heard whenever she said anything.

'You should ask Madame Letsworth if you can move to our dorm,' said Hannah after breakfast.

But when Emily asked, Madame Letsworth shook her head. 'If I let you move then everyone will want to swap around. I'm sorry, Emily, but the answer is no.'

Emily walked away, dejected. It looked like she was stuck with the Snow Foxes and that was that.

Over the next few days, the rest of the Snow Foxes continued to ignore Emily. She spent all her spare time in the Frost Fairies dorm. Tilda and Alice, the other two girls in Frost Fairies, were also really friendly. The five of them had a massive snowball fight one day, and, after tea on

Thursday, Alice, who was friends with the sylphs who looked after the huskies in the kennels, asked if they could all go on an evening sledge ride. It was brilliant!

The sledges were pulled by a team of huskies, each driven by an ice sylph. They raced across the frozen land, throwing up clouds of snow crystals as they were pulled through pine forests and past small villages with twinkling lights.

As Emily snuggled down under the thick blankets on the sledge, she wondered about the land they were passing through. Why did the ice sylphs need a human girl to help them, and what was the Ice Princess going to have to do? She longed to see more of the land, but there wasn't much time for exploring because every spare minute was spent practising for the competition.

On Saturday, the day before the competition, Emily got up early and went to the rink to practise. The frost fairies were smoothing over the ice, and two of them flew over and landed on her shoulders, their wings fluttering.

Emily smiled at them. They chattered to her in their high-pitched voices. She couldn't understand what they were saying, but she liked having them there. She put on her boots, warmed up and got on to the ice. The frost fairies fluttered away.

Push and glide, push and glide . . .

Emily set off round the rink, her arms out, her chin up, her eyes fixed straight ahead. She skated faster and felt the urge to jump. Kicking her left toe into the ice, she pushed herself into the air from her right leg. Drawing her arms to her chest, she crossed her ankles together and spun round. She landed elegantly – a perfect single toe loop.

Smiling in delight, she glided on. Her skating had really improved over the week. She loved it when she did the jumps and spins and spirals she had been learning and got them right. *I've got to decide*, she thought. *Do I do the easy routine or the hard one?*

Emily wanted to do the hard one, to do all the more difficult jumps and spins. But then she heard Camilla's voice in her head: *You'll just look stupid . . .*

She could just imagine Camilla and the other Snow Foxes laughing at her if she fell over lots in the competition.

No, I should just be sensible, she thought. *I don't want to make a total idiot of myself. I'll do the easy one.*

She started to practise her easy routine. She skated round the rink and then turned and went backwards. When she got to the point where she would have done a toe loop, she did a simple turn instead.

'What are you doing?' Emily looked round. Hannah and Molly were standing at the side of the rink, watching.

'My routine,' Emily called.

'But what about the jumps and spins?' asked Molly, coming on to the ice.

Emily took a breath. 'I don't think I'll do them. I still fall over quite a lot and I

don't want to do a routine that makes me look really dumb so I think I'll stick to the easy version.'

'But you were doing so well,' Hannah protested.

'I know.' Emily shrugged. 'But . . . but I just don't think I should do it.'

'Forget what you think,' Hannah said. 'What do you *feel*? Deep down?'

Emily hesitated.

'You *want* to do all the jumps and spins and spirals you've been practising, Em,' said Molly. 'I know you do.'

Emily nodded. 'You're right,' she admitted.

'Don't let other people put you off then,' said Hannah as if she could read Emily's thoughts about Camilla. 'You have to listen to your heart when you're skating. My coach at home is always saying that.'

'Hannah's right. If it doesn't work out, so what?' Molly took Emily's hands. 'The teachers won't think any the worse of you; they'll just be pleased you've tried your best, and even if you fall over a hundred times, we'll still be your friends. If you don't try, I bet you'll hate yourself and wish you had.'

Emily looked from one to the other. She knew they wouldn't tell her to do the hard routine if they thought she'd look silly, and they were right – she really did want to do it.

She made up her mind and grinned. 'OK. I'll do the hard routine after all!'

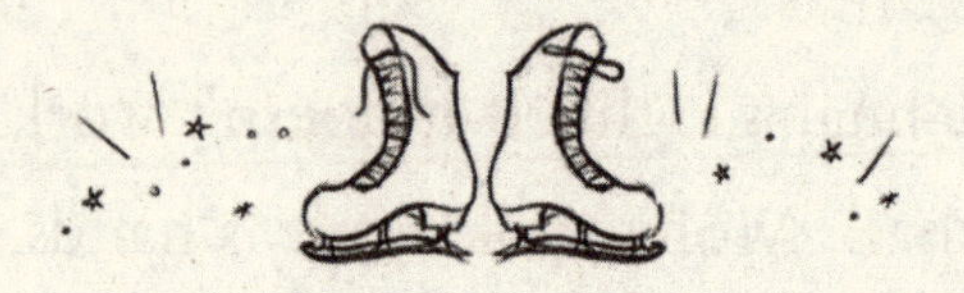

Chapter Nine

Camilla's Revenge

Deciding to skate the hard routine was only one part of the battle. Later that day, Emily had to face Camilla.

'You're not going to do those jumps in your routine tomorrow, are you?' Camilla asked as they all practised their routines before supper.

Emily lifted her chin high. 'Yes, I am.'

'You'll fall and look like an idiot.'

Emily thought about Molly and Hannah. She wasn't going to let Camilla bully her out of her decision. 'Well, I'm going to try.'

Camilla's eyes hardened. 'I don't think you should.'

Emily took a deep breath. This was so hard, but she wasn't going to be pushed around by Camilla any more. 'I don't care what you think!'

Camilla stared at her as if she couldn't believe what she was hearing. Emily's legs felt wobbly, but she met Camilla's gaze. She wasn't going to give in. She knew she was right to do the routine she had chosen.

'You'll be sorry about this, Emily Walker,' Camilla told her angrily.

Emily shrugged and with her heart pounding she hurried off to find Molly and Hannah.

At suppertime, Emily saw Camilla and the other Snow Foxes whispering and looking in her direction as if they were planning something. She didn't want to go back to the dorm that night, but she knew she had to. Walking slowly and feeling a bit sick, she headed from the

Frost Fairies dorm back down to the Snow Foxes dorm. As she got to the corridor, Camilla's words rang in her ears: *You'll be sorry about this.*

What had Camilla meant by that?

Just then, Amanda came hurrying up the stairs. Emily thought about the trick Camilla was playing on her. 'Amanda, wait a moment!' Emily said.

Amanda stopped and turned to look at her. 'What is it?'

'You know Camilla's been helping you with your routine?' Emily said hurriedly.

Amanda nodded.

'Well . . .' Emily took a deep breath. 'She's not really helping you. She's trying to make you look stupid.'

'Don't be silly. She's my friend,' said Amanda. 'I'm going to see her now.'

'She isn't your friend,' said Emily. 'She's telling you to do stuff that makes your routine look worse.'

'You don't know anything about it, Emily,' Amanda said dismissively. 'You don't even have ice-skating lessons at home!' She walked away and pushed open the door of the Snow Foxes dorm. The next minute there was a splash, a clatter and a piercing shriek!

Emily gasped and ran forward. Amanda was standing just inside the doorway and she was soaked through! A bucket lay at her feet. It had obviously been balanced on top of the door and had fallen down, spilling water all over her as she walked in. Camilla, Tess, Helena and Clare were staring at Amanda in shock.

'We thought Emily was about to come in, not you!' Tess gasped.

Camilla and the others burst out laughing. Emily stared. It was horrible knowing the others had been planning to play the trick on her and she couldn't help feeling a bit sorry for Amanda.

'Stop laughing!' Amanda shouted furiously, looking at Camilla.

'But you look so . . . so . . . so *funny*!' Camilla couldn't contain her giggles.

'I'm all wet!' Amanda cried. She got crosser and crosser, which made the others laugh even more. 'Stop it! Stop it! Stop it!' she screamed.

'Whatever is going on here?' a sharp voice snapped.

The laughter died instantly.

Madame Letsworth appeared in the

doorway and looked at Amanda and then at the water all over the floor. She glared at the girls in the dorm. 'Would anyone care to explain?' she said icily.

There wasn't a trace of laughter on any of the girls' faces now.

Camilla swallowed and stood up. 'It . . . it was just a joke.'

'I do not think it is very funny!' Madame Letsworth snapped. 'There is now water all over the floor and all over Emily's bed. Amanda, be quiet!'

Amanda's wails faded to snivels.

'Go and get changed and dry your hair.'

Amanda glared at Camilla and the others and hurried away.

Madame Letsworth looked round at Emily. 'Did you have anything to do with this, Emily?'

Emily quickly shook her head.

'Well, your bed is far too wet for you to sleep in tonight. Get your things and go to the Frost Fairies dorm and sleep in the spare bed there tonight.'

Emily caught her breath in delight.

'I am not pleased with the rest of you, not pleased at all. I expect more than this from my students. I want you to fetch mops from the cleaning cupboard and I

am going to stand here while you clear up this mess, and then you will be going to bed straight away with no talking at all.'

Madame Letsworth waited while Emily gathered up her pyjamas and clothes for the next day and the others fetched the mops. Leaving them clearing up the mess with very fed-up expressions on their faces, Emily ran up the stairs to the Frost Fairies dorm.

'I can sleep here tonight!' she gasped, bursting in.

'What? How?' exclaimed Molly.

Five minutes and an excited explanation later, Emily was unpacking her things. It was lovely to be out of the Snow Foxes dorm. She brushed her hair and teeth with the others and then got into the spare bed.

'I wish I could sleep here every night!'

'I wish you could too,' said Molly.

'Me three,' said Hannah.

'Me four,' said Alice.

'Me five!' said Tilda. They all giggled and then said goodnight. Alice turned off the light. Hannah was in the bed next to Emily's.

'Are you nervous about tomorrow?' she whispered through the dark.

'Yes,' Emily whispered back. 'But I'm excited as well.'

'You'll be brilliant, Emily,' Molly said from the bed next to Hannah's. 'We all will!'

Emily smiled happily and went to sleep.

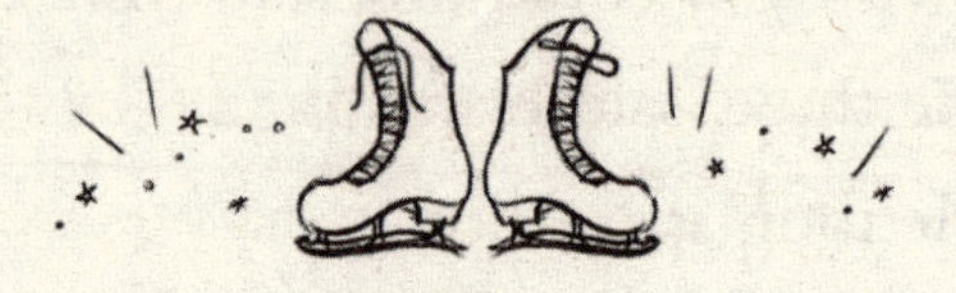

Chapter Ten

The Competition!

The next day there was an excited buzz in the air as the girls prepared for the competition. They all had a final practice with their music and then got ready. They were allowed to put make-up on as well. Emily wore blue eyeshadow and mascara and dusted silver powder over her cheeks.

The girls had been told they would be skating in three groups. The Frost Fairies dorm would go first, then the Ice Owls and finally the Snow Foxes. The competition was being judged by the three ice-skating teachers. The teachers all sat at a table and at the end of each round they agreed a mark and told the frost fairies who were sitting beside them. The frost fairies then fluttered up and formed the score in the air.

It was a very exciting competition to watch. Hannah did a brilliant routine. She skated effortlessly, gliding on the ice to beautiful music and landing all her jumps, looking graceful and elegant. She went into the lead. Molly tried to do some really difficult combinations of double jumps. She fell over twice, but didn't mind, and the rest of her routine was full of energy and fire. Amanda, who wasn't speaking to Camilla any more, toned down her routine and didn't overact. She was good and went into third place with the second place going to Heather, another girl from Ice Owls, who was a beginner like Emily but who did a very simple but expressive routine. After every routine the dragons in the music box popped up to clap their paws.

As Emily watched everyone go before her, she got more and more excited. At last, it was time for the Snow Foxes to go to the changing area where they would wait to be called on to the rink. Emily tucked in some loose strands of hair, checked that the laces on her boots were tied tightly and then waited, heart pounding, for her turn.

Please let me just get through it OK, she

thought. *Please let me not fall over too many times.*

Her hands were sweating and her stomach felt full of fluttering butterflies.

Tess was the first of the Snow Foxes to go on to the ice. She fell on one of her jumps, a single axel.

'See,' Camilla said, coming up behind Emily. 'If Tess fell, you're bound to.'

Tess got up from the ice, but the fall had shaken her and she limited the difficulty on the rest of her routine.

Camilla was on next. She skated to the centre of the rink, her chin up, a broad smile on her face. Her whole body language said '*Look at me*'. And she *was* good. When she started, Emily couldn't take her eyes off her. Camilla skated really well. She had chosen cat-like music and she jumped and spun and arched her back like a cat. She came skating off the ice, smiling smugly.

'Well done,' Emily said generously.

Camilla gave her a triumphant look. 'Beat that if you can!'

Emily stared after her as Camilla put on her skate guards and flounced away. Anger surged through her. *OK*, Emily thought determinedly, gritting her teeth, *I will!*

The score went up and everyone clapped again. Camilla had gone into the lead. But Emily didn't have time to think about Camilla any longer. It was her turn!

Taking her skate guards off, she stepped on to the glistening white ice. She skated to the centre of the rink and stood in her beginning pose, head down, arms slightly behind her like a bird's wings, left foot crossed behind the right. She felt excited, but also calm and very determined. Emily knew her routine was nothing like as technical as Camilla's, but if the judges wanted expression and dancing from the heart then that was what she was going to give them!

As the first few bars of the music flooded out, Emily blocked everything else from her mind, took a deep breath and began to skate.

At first, her feet felt heavy, but then the music seemed to flow through her, taking her over, just as it did when she was dancing off the ice. Emily could feel it building, getting louder, carrying her on. This was it. Her first jump. Increasing her speed, she remembered everything she had learnt that week. Head up, arms out, tap the ice with her left foot. *I can do this, I can do this*, she thought.

Emily leapt upwards, crossing her arms over her chest and spinning round, for a moment feeling completely weightless and free. She landed on her right foot and the music carried her on into a spiral, her leg held high, her balance perfect, and then into a sit spin. She remembered her routine perfectly, hardly having to think about what to do next, skating in perfect time to the music. Emily finished with a final spin, coming to a graceful stop, arms fully extended up above her head. There was a moment's pause and then everyone started clapping.

She beamed in relief. She'd done it! While she had been skating, she had been lost in her own world, but now she could see everyone. Hannah and Molly were on their feet cheering. The others were all clapping hard. The judges were smiling.

Happiness flooded through her. She hadn't fallen. She hadn't looked silly. She'd tried her hardest and it felt brilliant! She headed off the ice, smiling in delight.

The other Snow Foxes turned away

from her, but Hannah and Molly came running over. 'That was amazing!' cried Hannah. 'You were so expressive.'

'Just fantastic!' exclaimed Molly.

'The marks are going up!' said Hannah as the frost fairies fluttered up from the table.

Emily looked at the marks and gasped. She had beaten Camilla!

'You're in the lead!' shrieked Molly.

Emily could hardly believe it. She watched in a daze as the final two skaters performed and, at the end of it, she still had the most points. She had won the competition!

Madame Letsworth, Madame Li and Monsieur Carvallio skated on to the ice and called Emily on.

Everyone clapped. Emily noticed the

Snow Foxes were all applauding very grudgingly, but all her friends in the Frost Fairies dorm made up for that by cheering loudly. 'Well done, Emily,' Madame Letsworth said.

'Your routine was excellent,' said Monsieur Carvallio. 'It showed real feeling and expression. You have also shown great improvement this week. No

one has worked harder or tried more, and you showed great courage in attempting the routine you did, so I am delighted you have won.'

'You should be very proud of yourself. Well done, Emily,' agreed Madame Li, handing her a pair of perfect white skates.

Emily stroked the soft leather in delight. They were the most beautiful skates she had ever seen, with silver laces and golden fastenings.

'As the winner of the first competition, you can ask for one thing,' said Madame Letsworth. 'And, if we can grant it, you will have it. So, what is it to be? A sleigh ride maybe? A midnight feast? A new ice-skating dress?'

Emily shook her head. She knew exactly

what she wanted. 'Can I move into the Frost Fairies dorm, please?' she asked.

Madame Letsworth looked surprised. 'Switch dorms?'

'Yes, please.' Emily held her breath.

'I have already told you, Emily, changing dorms is not possible . . .' The headteacher's face softened into a smile. 'In *most* cases. But if that is what you want then you shall have it as winner of the competition.'

Emily's heart leapt. *Oh, wow!* she thought.

Molly and Hannah were waiting for her as she skated off the ice.

'I can't believe you're going to be in our dorm!' said Molly, hugging her. 'It'll be so cool!'

'Just brilliant!' exclaimed Hannah.

'No more people not talking to me.' Emily looked round. Camilla had already marched off and the Snow Foxes had followed her. 'No more tricks being played.'

Amanda came over. 'Well done, Emily. And . . .' She hesitated. 'Thank you for telling me about Camilla,' she said stiffly. 'I'm sorry I didn't listen.'

Emily smiled at her. 'That's OK. You looked really good today.'

Amanda tossed her head. 'I know. I mean, obviously they were trying to encourage the beginners so that's why you won. But that's OK,' she said as if she thought she was being generous. 'Congratulations.' She walked off.

Molly spluttered. 'I can't believe she just said that!'

'Oh, forget it,' said Hannah. 'It's just Amanda. It doesn't matter.'

Emily nodded. She didn't want to waste the moment thinking about Amanda. 'This has been a brilliant week!'

'I wonder what the competition will be next week,' said Molly eagerly.

'And if we'll find out anything more about being the Ice Princess,' Hannah added.

Emily sighed happily and looked at the ice rink. It was empty of people now, but in her mind she could still feel what it had been like to be out there, skating to music, gliding and jumping. She'd only been at the Magic Ice-skating Academy for a week and already she had learnt so much and done so many things. *What will happen next week? What will we be doing?* she thought.

The first adventure was over, but another one was about to begin!

With Thanks To . . .

There are so many people who deserve thanks for this series: Lindsey Heaven who first came up with the idea and who has cared passionately about the series from the start; Philippa Milnes-Smith for her constant support, encouragement and advice; Jessica and Michele Holland for talking about skating to me and for reading through the books, checking the skating details (any mistakes are all mine and I freely admit there is some artistic licence in there!); Suzanne Duxbury for going above and beyond the call of best friendship in looking after six children for far too much of the time during a rainy week in Devon while I finished *White Skate Wishes*, and who is always there for me the rest of the time too; Emma Purcell for listening, for the e-mails, for making me laugh and for keeping me sane; Steve Cole who helped with this series from the very earliest stages and who gave so much with useful advice, brilliant ideas and encouragement, despite his own mad schedule; Lee Weatherly who has been my 'girl' reader, whose instincts are so close to my own – thank you so much for all your involvement and support; Dave Gatward for the daily optimism, endless enthusiasm, for producing articles on skiing at the drop of a hat and for the icicle snakes and snowball mice – brilliant! And the biggest thanks of all to Peter who puts up with so much – looking after me, the dogs and the children when I am busy writing – thank you for that and for all the brainstorming, map-drawing and reading, but most of all for always believing and never letting me give up. You are truly wonderful!

Do you dream of becoming an Ice Princess?

Have you ever wanted to go to a REAL Skating School?

All readers of *Skating School* get FREE membership to the National Ice Skating Association's Skate UK programme!

Skate UK will help you to learn all the moves and basic skills you need to become a true Ice Princess! It's all about fun and continuous movement and is taught in groups, so why not share your love of *Skating School* with your friends and bring them too?

To get your free membership, go to
www.iceskating.org.uk/skatingschool
and enter the secret password: **Twirl**.

Skate UK is taught by licensed NISA coaches and can be assisted by trained Programme Assistants.

For full terms and conditions visit:

www.lindachapman.co.uk

www.iceskating.org.uk/skatingschool

Do you want to enter super competitions, get sneak previews and download lots of *Skating School* fun?

Get YOUR skates on

join the

Sparkle Club

today!

lindachapman.co.uk

Just enter this secret password:

The Land of Ice and Winter is waiting for you ...

Design your own ice-skating dress!

The tiny frost fairies have been working overtime designing the beautiful dresses for the girls to wear in the Ice-skating Academy competitions.

Using this dress as a template, the fairies need you to draw the most magical ice-skating outfit you can think of. Every month one lucky winner will receive a magical *Skating School* goody bag!

Send your drawing
with your name and address to:

Skating School Competition, Puffin Marketing, 80 Strand, London WC2R 0RL

Or e-mail them to: **skatingschool@uk.penguingroup.com**

Welcome back to the magical Land of Ice and Winter

... a world where all your dreams come true!

A brand-new

Skating School series

Coming soon!

Hi there,

I hope you've enjoyed reading about the adventures of the girls who go to the Magic Ice-skating Academy. I love writing them all down! Wouldn't it be amazing to go to the Land of Ice and Winter and see all the creatures who live there? Can you imagine holding an actual ice dragon or talking to a frost fairy?

Sometimes readers write to me and ask about my life. Being a writer is the best job ever. I live in a cottage in a village with my family and two dogs – a Bernese mountain dog and a golden retriever. I spend my days writing and going to visit schools and libraries to talk about writing.

I always think I'm really lucky because I get to spend my days writing about magic – mermaids, unicorns, stardust spirits, genies and now the Land of Ice and Winter. If you love them too then why not go to **www.lindachapman.co.uk** and join the Sparkle Club? It's my online fan club with loads of activities and downloads, and you can only get to it by using the secret password at the back of this book. Have fun!

Love,

Linda

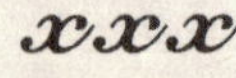